Name

Address

ILLUSTRATED BY

MARIA MURRAY

TONY HICKEY

THE MATCHLESS MICE

IN SPACE

THE CHILDREN'S PRESS

First published in 1986 by
The Children's Press
90 Lower Baggot Street, Dublin 2

© Text: Tony Hickey
© Illustrations: The Children's Press

ISBN 0 947962 09 3 cased
ISBN 0 947962 10 7 paper

To my Mother
who hates all mice except, of course,
The Matchless Mice

Origination by M & J Graphics
Printed in Ireland by Mount Salus Press

Contents

1
Whose Cottage?

All winter long, the countryside around the cottage where the Matchless Mice now lived with Fred, the cat, and the other mice from Mangold Mansion was covered with snow.

For weeks on end, it was far too cold to go out. This was a good thing in a way, for it gave everyone a chance to settle down in their new home.

The Matchless Mice and Fred moved into the front room of the cottage. It wasn't nearly as grand as the drawing-room at Mangold Mansion and, at first, everyone was worried that Grandfather Matchless might not like it. But then to everyone's delight he was heard to say to old Crumbs Kitchen, 'I think I'm happier here than ever I was in the old place. It's all so much cosier somehow.'

Old Crumbs nodded his head in agreement. 'That's just what Mrs. Crumbs and I were saying the other day. We couldn't be more pleased with the way things have worked out.'

Old Crumbs and Mrs. Crumbs Kitchen had been given the kitchen, which seemed only right for mice of that name.

'And we aren't the only ones who enjoy living here,' old Crumbs continued. 'Isn't that so, Alta Attic?'

Alta Attic stuck her head out of what had been a storage space up under the roof. 'Oh, you've hit it there all right. I'm as snug as a bug in a rug up here. When I think how lonely I was all those years on the top floor of Mangold Mansion, I don't know why we didn't move long ago.'

The Always Hungries, who now lived in the larder, squeaked, 'We owe it all to Grandfather Matchless and his little grandmouse Scratch and, of course, Fred, the cat.'

Grandfather Matchless smiled benignly. 'Don't forget that old Crumbs helped as well.'

'Oh now, now,' said old Crumbs modestly, 'I only did what had to be done.' But he was so delighted by the praise that he blushed, causing his fur to turn pink.

Fred and Scratch glanced at each other. Everything was going very well.

Then Flap, Scratch's mother, said, 'I wonder who used to live here before we did.'

'Now why do you ask that?' enquired Moaner, Scratch's father.

'Well, we know that the people who once lived in Mangold Mansion must have been very rich,' said Flap. 'But this place is so much smaller and it's in the middle of a field, miles from anywhere. And did you not notice it isn't nearly as dusty as Mangold Mansion used to be?'

Grandmother Matchless stopped what she was doing and said, 'But the country is never as dusty as the city.'

Flap nodded her head. 'I suppose that's true but all the same there's something about the place that I can't quite explain.'

'Does that mean you don't like it?' asked Fred.

'No, it's not exactly that I don't like it. I'd just like to know who lived here.'

'I think we'd be better off not worrying about things that don't concern us.' Grandfather's voice was rather sharp.

'Oh, I'm sorry, I didn't mean to upset anyone. I won't mention it again.'

And neither did she mention it again. Yet the other mice could not help thinking about what she had asked. Just who had lived in the cottage in the middle of the field? They began to look more carefully around the place.

So too did Fred. He noticed things like the cups and plates on the dresser. And the oil in the lamps on the table. And the curtains on the window.

Scratch noticed the sweeping brush behind the front door. And they both noticed how Grandfather and Grandmother Matchless would slip away and talk very quietly and seriously with old Crumbs and Mrs. Crumbs Kitchen. Yet if anyone came close enough to the four elderly mice to be able to hear what was being said, the elderly mice would immediately stop talking.

'There's something up,' little Scratch said to Fred. 'And I think I might know what it is.'

'I think I might know as well. It has to do with your mother wondering who used to live here. I think the question she should have asked was not who used to live here but who STILL lives here. Lots of city people have country cottages that they use during the holidays.'

Scratch shivered. 'Which means that, if this place belongs to humans, they might come back in the summer. And they might not like mice.'

'They might not like cats either! If only there was some way we could find out,' sighed Fred.

'The animals at the farmyard would know.'

Fred brightened up at once. 'Of course they would.'

'Let's go and talk to Grandfather.'

They found Grandfather Matchless staring out of the front room window, and they climbed up beside him.

Grandfather tried to smile at them as he spoke.

'Oh, so there you are. And from the look of your faces you have something to say to me.'

'We think we know why you and Grandmother and the Crumbs Kitchens are worried,' said Scratch. 'It's about what might happen in the fine weather.'

'And humans come here,' added Fred.

Grandfather's smile faded. 'So we haven't been so clever about keeping things to ourselves.'

'Fred and I have an idea,' said Scratch. 'As soon as the snow melts we thought we'd go and talk to the animals in the farmyard.'

'If it turns out that humans do still come here,' continued Fred, 'the animals will surely find us somewhere else to move to.'

'Brilliant!' smiled Grandfather. 'It couldn't have been better if I'd thought of it myself. But mind now, not a word to the others. We don't want to upset anyone before we have to and maybe we have nothing at all to worry about.'

After that talk, Grandmother and Grandfather Matchless didn't seem nearly so worried. They no longer had long serious conversation with the Crumbs Kitchens. Instead they laughed and joked and even joined in games of *Hunt the Cheese* and *Climb the Table Leg,* while outside the cold north wind rattled the window panes.

Time passed quickly. The days became brighter and longer. The snow melted. The land dried out. Daffodils shoved green shoots up through the earth. Bluebells appeared in the woods. The sun grew stronger and stronger, until one morning Fred and Scratch woke to find the front room filled with warm golden light.

They both knew at once that it was the beginning of

spring, the perfect day to go to the farmyard. They rushed outside where the sky was so blue and the breeze so warm that they did a dance of delight. Then Scratch sang a song that came into his mind as if by magic.

It's Spring!
It's Spring!
Hear the bluebells ring,
Hear the robins sing.
It's time to go
Out walking

The song was so happy and the words so easy to remember that every mouse in the cottage came out and joined in. Then they danced until they collapsed, exhausted from so much exercise.

After a pause, Scratch picked himself up and went over to where Grandfather lay. 'Grandfather,' he said as quietly as he could. 'I think it's time for the visit.'

Flap, whose hearing was remarkably good even for a mouse, at once sat up. 'Visit? What visit?'

'Just to the farmyard,' said Grandfather. 'It seems only right to pay the animals a visit. They've been very good to us. Scratch might even invite them back here.'

'But does Scratch know where the farmyard is?' asked Flap. 'Is it safe for him to go away from the cottage?'

'Of course it's safe,' replied Grandfather. 'Fred is going too. Scratch can ride on his back. No harm will come to them. They'll easily find the farmyard.'

'Well, all right.' Flap sounded reluctant. 'But they're not to be gone too long.'

'We'll be as quick as we can,' Scratch promised. Then he jumped up on Fred's back and off the two of them went across the field before Flap could say another word.

2

The Mouse from Glitter

Scratch looked out between Fred's ears and said, 'This is almost as exciting as the time we were chased by the Tough Cat Gang.'

A cold shiver ran down Fred's spine at the mere mention of the Gang. 'I most sincerely hope nothing like that will happen here,' he said as he jumped into the next field, which was much smaller than the one they had just crossed and had a river flowing along one side of it.

'That must be the river we travelled along last Christmas in order to get to the cottage,' exclaimed Scratch. 'It looks very different now.'

And indeed the river did look completely different. At Christmas it had been frozen so hard that Fred had been able to pull all the mice along it in a big box. Now on the first day of spring it shone and sparkled, almost humming as it flowed along.

'Gosh, it's so lovely,' sighed Scratch. 'If only we could go for a swim!'

'A swim! Are you mad? I'm a cat, not a fish. Anyway, I don't think mice can swim.'

'Maybe that's because they never get a chance.'

'Well you're not going to get a chance now. I'm responsible for you and we're supposed to be on our way to the farmyard!'

'Well we can go to the farmyard and talk about swimming at the same time,' argued Scratch. 'If we follow the river, it'll bring us to where we set sail on the raft.'

'That's true,' agreed Fred, 'but, please, no more talk about swimming.'

But Scratch was no longer listening to Fred. Instead he had jumped down off Fred's back and was running towards the water.

Fred ran after him. 'You're not going to do something stupid, are you? You could get cramp. You could be swept right down to the waterfall and then who would save you?'

But Scratch did not jump into the water. Instead he pointed to a bright shining object in the middle of the river. 'What's that?'

Fred shielded his eyes against the glare of the sun. 'I don't know ... unless it's some kind of tin can.'

A light flashed from the middle of the object.

There was a moment's pause. Then the same flashes of light were repeated.

'It's sending out signals,' cried Scratch.

Suddenly the shining metal object rose up out of the water and moved towards them.

'It's a spaceship,' Scratch yelled with delight. 'It's a SPACESHIP!'

Fred realized that Scratch was right. Fred knew about spaceships. When he'd been a supermarket cat he'd heard the staff in the stock room talking about spaceships and how they might invade the earth. He had even seen a picture of a spacecraft in a comic that had fallen on the floor. Dozens of men with green and yellow faces were getting out of it.

But the spaceship coming across the river looked nothing like the one in the comic. It was more like a pale yellow banana and was far too small to hold even one green-faced man, much less dozens of them. All the same,

13

Fred decided it was no time to take chances.

'Come on!' he urged. 'Let's get out of here!'

But Scratch didn't move. 'I want to see what's going to happen next . . . . Besides we'd never be able to run faster than a spaceship. They can travel hundreds of miles per hour.'

By now the spaceship was hovering directly above their heads and making a noise like an angry bee. Then slowly, very slowly, it came to rest on the river bank beside them. A panel in the side of the spaceship slid open. Out stepped the tiniest mouse that Scratch and Fred had ever see. She had huge blue eyes, bright yellow fur and was wearing a space suit the colour of silver. She bowed slightly to Fred and Scratch and said, 'Bleep, bleep, plong, plong, pingawinga.'

'Pardon?' said Scratch.

The strange mouse looked very surprised. 'You speak English? I thought on Mars you'd speak Martian.'

'Mars?' asked Fred. 'Do you mean the planet Mars, that's thousands and thousands of miles away?'

'Well, she hardly meant a Mars bar.'

'Please, Scratch, this is serious.' Fred spoke to the mouse from space again. 'This is not Mars. This is the planet Earth.'

'But if I am on earth I am completely lost,' the space mouse said. 'And I have a very important message for the mice on Mars from the mice of Glitter.'

'Is that where you come from then?' asked Scratch. 'Glitter?'

'That is correct. My name is Gladys.'

'Gladys?' put in Fred. 'That's a Welsh name, isn't it?'

'On Glitter it means , "She who can be relied upon",' replied Gladys. 'And so many creatures are relying on me. Oh but you, Master Cat, who seem to be so well versed in the secrets of the universe, must help me.'

For a second, Fred didn't realize that Gladys was talking

14

to him. But before he could explain that all he knew about the universe came from a comic book, Scratch said, 'Of course Fred will help you. We will both help you.'

'Oh, thank you... Now we must leave at once.'

She pointed a tiny silver torch at Fred and Scratch. There was a dazzling flash of white light and a loud POP! When they could see properly again, Fred and Scratch were no longer standing on the river bank. Instead, they were sitting inside the spaceship.

Fred was puzzled. 'I don't understand. How can we be inside the spaceship, when the spaceship is only the same size as Scratch?'

'I used the size torch,' explained Gladys. 'White light for small. Blue beam for large. Please prepare for take-off.'

'Take-off to where?' Fred demanded as seat belts came out of the arms of the seats and fastened himself and Scratch tightly into place. 'Where are we going?'

'To wherever you suggest. It is not advisable to stay too long in one place in case we attract too much attention.'

'But will what looks like a banana flying through the air not attract a lot of attention?' asked Fred.

'You are right, of course,' replied Gladys. 'We must press the invisibility button.'

She leaned forward and pressed one of the buttons on the control panel, where pink and green and white lights were flashing on and off.

'It's a lovely spaceship,' Scratch was looking around at the pale blue walls. 'Are we invisible now?'

'We are!'

'And small as well,' thought Fred. He didn't care for the way things were going. He liked it even less when he looked out of the window and saw the river and the fields and Grandfather and old Crumbs sitting outside the cottage in the bright sunlight.

Quickly he whispered to Scratch, 'Have you forgotten that we are supposed to be finding out if humans still live in the cottage?'

'Of course I haven't forgotten that,' Scratch whispered back, 'but we have to help Gladys.'

'But how can we help her? We know nothing about space travel. If she finds out we're wasting her time, she might turn nasty. She might leave us small.'

'Of course she won't do that. She's nice. I like her.'

Gladys turned to Scratch and smiled at him. 'Have you decided in which direction we must go?'

'The city would be best. They're bound to know about space travel in the city.'

'Are you suggesting we ask HUMANS?' Fred asked in horror.

16

'No, no, of course not. We'll have to find out for ourselves. But that should be easy since we're invisible. But Gladys hasn't yet told us why it's so important for her to reach the mice on Mars. In fact she hasn't even told us how she became a space mouse.'

'Oh, that is not hard to explain,' said Gladys. 'The planet Glitter belongs to the animals. There is a power in the rocks there that we have learned to use. We built canals and bridges and grew food so that everyone has plenty to eat. We even learned how to build spaceships. And the mice of Glitter were particularly good at flying them, so naturally every mouse, when old enough, learned how to fly a spaceship.'

'How wonderful!' said Scratch.

'Yes,' Gladys agreed. 'We had a wonderful life. Then one day a fleet of strange spacecraft landed on Glitter. They belonged to the Creatures from beyond the Sun.'

'Did they have hideous faces?' asked Fred, remembering the pictures in the comic book.

'Yes, they did. Oh, but from where have you acquired such knowledge?'

'Well it's not exactly knowledge. But, please, continue with your story.'

'The Creatures from Beyond the Sun said they needed somewhere new to live. The water had dried up on their planet. There was plenty of room on Glitter so we made them welcome. But they did not wish just to share our planet. They wanted to take it away from us. They began to make slaves of the animals and force them to work long hours. Soon only the mice were left free. But we were not strong enough to fight the Creatures by ourselves. So it was decided that we should seek help from the mice on Mars whom we had visited on several occasions.

17

I had the honour to be chosen for this mission. While the other mice pretended to be going about their daily lives, I managed to escape without being noticed. If only I hadn't ended up in England by mistake.'

'But you're not in England,' said Fred. 'You're in Ireland.'

'Ach, cén fáth nach bhfuilimid ag labhairt Gaeilge?' asked Gladys.

'She wants to know why we aren't speaking Irish,' whispered Scratch.

'Let's not go into that right now,' said Fred. 'Isn't that the city down there?'

Scratch looked out of the window. The river now flowed between stone walls and under bridges crowded with traffic and people.

'There's a place in the middle of the city called a university,' said Scratch. 'It's supposed to be full of clever people. Maybe we should go there and look for information. Could we go down a bit lower, please, Gladys?'

As Gladys reached for the correct handle, there was a loud thud! The spaceship was sent spinning through the air!

'What was that?' Fred cried out.

Scratch looked out the window again and saw a seagull hovering on a current of air. It had a puzzled look on its face and a slight dinge in its beak.

'A seagull must have flown into us,' said Scratch. 'Only of course it can't see us. Oh, but here it comes again.'

Gladys steered the spaceship out of the way just in time as the seagull nose-dived at where it hoped the spaceship would be. The seagull missed but the movement of the spaceship ruffled his feathers. The bird knew for certain now that there was something there, something he couldn't see. He flew backwards for a few yards and dived again.

Again he missed, and got ready for a third attempt.

From their perches on the buildings above the river, other seagulls became curious about what was happening. They screeched out, 'What are you at? What are you doing?'

'Something hit me,' the dinged seagull shrieked back. 'It's invisible but it's still there.'

'Invisible? Invisible?' A great raucous chorus filled the air as dozens of seagulls left the buildings to join in the hunt.

A red light began to flash on the control panel.

Gladys looked worried. 'That light means we have used too much power. We must land and rest. Otherwise, we will become visible and have to travel very slowly. We would be at the mercy of those birds.'

Far across the city, the sun danced on a great glass window. 'Could we travel as far as that?' Scratch asked.

'Yes, I think so. But why there!'

'Because I'm pretty certain that's the supermarket where Fred used to work,' said Scratch. 'We could rest in whatever is left of Mangold Mansion.'

Gladys carefully steered the spacecraft through the flock of birds, who were now flying around in a very disorganized way. They even crashed into each other and shouted things like, 'Watch what you're doing!' and 'Just exactly where do you think you're going?' In fact, they were so busy being rude to each other that this time not even the dinged seagull felt the air move as the spaceship zoomed off across the city towards the supermarket and Mangold Mansion.

3

Encounters of a Close Kind

The supermarket was surrounded by parked cars. Delivery vans unloaded fresh supplies. A huge grey cat lay sleeping on the flat roof of the main building.

'That must be the cat who got your job,' chuckled Scratch. 'Wouldn't he be surprised to know you're up here in a spaceship?'

'I'm a bit surprised to be up here myself,' said Fred

Then they both fell silent for they could now see all that remained of Mangold Mansion and its garden. Only the steps up to the front door were still in place. Everything else had been reduced to a pile of rubble, on top of which was a block of granite with the date '1900'.

All the trees and shrubs in the garden had been uprooted and shoved into a pile, waiting to be taken away. New houses would soon be built. Then only Fred and the mice would remember Mangold Mansion.

Fred brushed away a tear with his paw.

So too did Scratch, and when he spoke his voice sounded very shaky, but he managed to say, 'Gladys, why don't you land in the roots of the old oak-tree?'

The spaceship fitted very neatly into the place suggested by Scratch. Gladys turned off the controls and opened the sliding panel. Fred and Scratch stepped out. They were no taller than the smallest twig on the ground.

'Well, I'll be an educated pigeon,' a familiar voice called. 'Did you shrink in the wash or what?'

Fred and Scratch looked up. Perched on a branch

above their heads was the magpie, his head twisting from one side to the other, his bright eyes shining with curiosity.

Gladys came to the door of the spaceship and looked out.

The magpie's eyes became even brighter. Fred suddenly remembered stories of how magpies loved to steal bright, shining things. Quickly he jumped in front of Gladys. 'Don't you try any of your tricks here,' he said warningly.

'As though I would,' said the magpie. 'And anyway if I was interested in collecting mice from space, my nest would be full of them hours ago.'

'What do you mean?' asked Scratch.

'Well, there are at least four of them flying around. I sent them to Arán in the Gaeltacht.'

But before the magpie could give directions, there was a great rustling noise among the branches of the uprooted oak-tree. Then the branches parted. A pair of bright green eyes appeared.

'It's the Creatures from Beyond the Sun,' Fred thought.

The branches parted further. The green eyes were now surrounded by marmalade-coloured fur.

'Tough Cat Gang!' the magpie called out in alarm. 'Tough Cat Gang! I'm off! I'm off!'

A great paw swiped at the magpie as he left the branch. Fred and the mice just had time to step back into the shadows of the roots as the branches parted even further.

The magpie was right. The green eyes, the marmalade fur and the great paw belonged to Jamser, one of the leaders of the Tough Cat Gang.

Jamser looked carefully all around. Then, looking over his shoulder, he called out, 'Nixer, are you sure you saw something moving around in here?'

21

'Of course I am, Jamser.' A second cat, black as night, came into view. This was Nixer, the other leader of the Tough Cat Gang.

'Well, all I've been able to find is that old nuisance of a magpie,' complained Jamser. 'I'm beginning to think it's a waste of time coming around here. I think Fred and his mice friends buzzed off after the fright we gave them.'

Scratch thought indignantly, 'It was Fred and me who gave YOU the fright.'

'Well, all the same, 'said Nixer,' we'll have one final search before we call it a day.' He began to rummage through the leaves and the branches.

'What'll we do?' whispered Scratch. 'Even if we get away, they'll find the spaceship.'

'I cannot use my weapon to harm other animals,' Gladys whispered back.

'If only we were our normal size,' sighed Fred softly.

'Or BIGGER!' said Scratch, as a wonderful idea came to him. 'Gladys, can you make us bigger?'

'Yes, of course,' said Gladys.

'Come on then!' Scratch grabbed Fred and Gladys by the paw. The three of them ran underneath Nixer and out into the middle of the wrecked garden.

Nixer yelled, 'They're still here. Come on! We'll catch them this time.'

Both cats jumped out of the fallen tree. Then they both fell backwards with loud miaows of terror as there, in front of their very eyes, giant versions of Fred and Scratch seemed to grow out of the ground.

'It's ... it's a what-you-may-call-it ...' said Nixer, '... a day nightmare.'

'But we both couldn't be having the same daymare,' gasped Jamser.

Together they began to back away from Fred and Scratch.

'It must be those fish bones we ate last night from the bin outside *The Gay Paree,*' Nixer said. 'French food never agrees with me.'

'Go home,' shouted Scratch. His voice boomed across the garden.

'*Both* of you go home!' added Fred. His voice was even louder than Scratch's. 'And don't ever come back here.'

'All right, all right,' said Nixer. 'We're going, we're going.' He and Jamser turned and ran out of sight as fast as they could. And they kept on running until they reached the old wrecked car in the back lane where they usually had gang meetings.

Nixer gasped for breath. 'How is that possible?' he asked. 'How can a cat and a mouse have grown that big?'

'Don't forget the time they came flying back from the country,' said Jamser.

'That was different,' Nixer replied. 'The skylarks helped them to do that. But who is helping them now is what I want to know?'

'It'd be nice to find out all right,' said Jamser. 'In fact, if we learned to do it ourselves we could rule the entire city in a matter of days.'

'Yeh, and it'd stop us being made a laughing stock of . . . if word got out how a cat and a mouse put the skids under us.'

Nixer left the wrecked car and smoothed down his ruffled fur. 'Come on,' he said. 'There's work to be done but we will have to be as quiet as shadows.'

They began to creep back towards the oak-tree.

4

Along the Animals' Highway

Scratch and Fred felt themselves shrink back to the same size as Gladys.

'I am sorry to have to reduce your size once more,' said Gladys, 'and to put an end to such a good joke, but it is essential that we find the other mice from Glitter.'

'How much longer does the spaceship need to rest?' asked Fred.

'It should be ready very soon now. It is just a question of letting the engines cool down. They seem to do that very quickly on earth. Also, unfortunately, they seem to use power more quickly.'

'Maybe that's because there's something wrong with them,' said Fred. 'Maybe that's how you lost your way.'

'Once I find the other mice from Glitter, everything will be all right,' said Gladys. 'Now, please, let us set out for the Gaeltacht.'

'The magpie left before he told us how to get there,' said Scratch.

'Ah, yes, but now he's back to give those instructions.' The bright-eyed bird was on the same branch of the oak tree. 'It's very simple. Fly towards the setting sun. You will cross the great river and see the mountain with the seven bends. Beyond that you'll see the great carved stone and the sea. In the shadow of that stone, you'll find the fort of the MacLeasas.'

Jamser and Nixer were just in time to hear what the magpie had said.

'Thank you very much, Mr. Magpie,' said Gladys, as she and Scratch and Fred climbed back into the spaceship. 'Oh, and please do not tell anyone where we have gone.'

'Who could possibly follow us?' Scratch asked, as the spaceship took off. 'At the speed we travel, no one could possibly catch us unless . . .' Scratch paused thoughtfully, 'unless there is something you haven't told us.'

'It is just a question of being careful,' said Gladys. 'If the mice from Glitter followed me to earth, there is always the chance that they too might have been followed.'

'By the Creatures from Beyond the Sun?' Scratch asked.

'Yes!' Gladys sounded tense.

'But did you not turn on the invisibility button when we left the oak-tree?' Fred asked.

'It uses so much power. I only like to press it in an emergency.'

'Well the sky looks clear enough now,' said Fred, 'apart from that rain cloud over there. It makes things dark.'

'We can fly above a rain cloud.' said Gladys, as she turned a handle on the control panel. The spaceship went up higher in the sky.

'That's funny!' said Scratch. 'The rain cloud seems to be as close to us as before. In fact, it seems to be changing shape. And colour as well.'

The rain cloud no longer looked like a rain cloud. The middle of it was bright purple. It began to divide into four separate parts. The four separate parts became four huge spaceships.

'It's the Creatures from Beyond the Sun!' cried Gladys.

'I'll bet they don't want to get into trouble with human beings,' said Scratch. 'Being small can be a great help to us. We can go places where they can't. Gladys, take us down as close as you can to the ground. We'll use the animals' highway for our escape.'

Gladys pulled the down handle as hard as she could.

The spaceship dropped like a stone out of the sky and into the cover of a thick hedge.

'That's great!' shouted Scratch.

'But what's the animals' highway?' asked Fred.

'This is it,' explained Scratch. 'Ireland is covered with hedges and ditches that the smaller wild animals use to get from one place to another.'

The ditch below the hedge was both dry and deep and perfect for the spaceship to travel along.

Overhead the four spaceships bleeped and buzzed while shrews and robins and sleepy hedgehogs stared in amazement at the flying banana. Prowling foxes became like statues. Stoats and weasels jumped out of the way and hid in crumbling walls.

Then suddenly where one ditch ended and another should have begun, there was a great gap.

'Where has the highway gone?' asked Gladys.

'I don't know.' Scratch sounded puzzled. 'The hedges are gone as well.'

'It must have to do with making fields larger,' said Fred. 'I seem to remember hearing about that at the supermarket. Hedges were being torn up.'

'Well, honest to goodness!' declared Scratch. 'Are we never to be safe anywhere? Not even on our own highway?'

Fred jumped suddenly. 'What's that?'

A strange noise was coming from the side of the ditch immediately beside them. Then the side of the ditch began to move and tremble. A great lump of earth fell out, just

26

missing the spaceship and leaving a gaping hole. Out of this hole, there walked none other than Arán from the Gaeltacht.

'Ó tá sibh anseo faoi dheireadh,' ar seisean. 'Táimíd ag fanacht oraibh ó mhaidin.'

'It's Arán!' cried Scratch. 'He's been waiting for us since this morning. Quick, Gladys, open the door.'

'But how did he know we were coming?' asked Fred. 'What does he mean by *we've* been waiting?'

'He means the mice from Glitter of course!' Scratch ran into the hole in the side of the ditch. A great tunnel stretched back into the darkness, and standing in the middle of the tunnel were four mice, all dressed like Gladys. Behind them were four banana-shaped spaceships.

Gladys pushed past Scratch and gave each of the four mice a big hug. They began to talk very quickly in a language that Fred and Scratch had never heard before.

'Must be Glitterish,' said Fred. 'But ask Arán how he met them.'

Quickly Arán told his story while Scratch translated.

'Bhíos ag siúl na trá.'

'I was walking along the seashore.'

'Go tobann thuirling ceithre spásarthach bheaga bhídeacha taobh liom.'

'Suddenly four tiny spaceships landed beside me.'

'Amach le ceithre luch ó Ghlitter ag fiafraí díom an raibh Gladys feicthe agam.'

'Out popped four mice from Glitter asking if I'd seen Gladys.'

'Díreach ansin, chualadar comhartha ar raidió Ghladys.'

'Just then, they heard a signal from Gladys's radio.'

'That must have been at the same time as we saw the blue light flashing on the river,' said Fred.

'Tá an ceart agat,' arsa Arán. 'Rinneamar iarracht "signal" a tabhairt ar ais ach níor furamar aon freagra. B'fhéidir go bhfuil rud éigin briste 'san spásárthach.'

'They tried to send a signal back but they got no answer. There must be something broken in the spaceship.'

'Ach b'fhéidir linn cloisint gach aon rud a bhí le rá agaibhse. Sin mar a bhî fhios againn cá raibh sibh.'

'But they were able to hear everything we said. That's how they knew where we were.'

'Then that's how the Creatures knew where we were as well,' said Fred excitedly. 'And they could be listening to us now.'

'No,' said Gladys who had come back to join them. 'The Creatures only speak and understand their own language. My friends here have told me that it was when the Creatures decided to count the mice on Glitter that they realized that I and my spaceship were missing. It was then that they set off after me. They probably managed to break my radio with one of their beams.'

'They probably did something to your controls as well,' said Scratch, 'to make you land on earth instead of on Mars. That could be why your engines have to rest so often!'

'But what do we do now?' asked Fred,' I don't hear the sound of their spaceship any longer, but they could still be waiting out there somewhere for us.'

Gladys smiled. 'Arán has thought of a brilliant plan, which he has explained to my four friends. We are indeed very pleased to be with not only the cleverest cat in all Ireland but the cleverest mouse as well.'

'Oh, indeed we are. Indeed we are.' The other four mice from Glitter began to bow and smile.

'Oh, but I have not told you my friends' names,' Gladys went on. 'Fred and Scratch, I would like you to meet... Count, Down, Rocket and Contact.'

'Our pleasure! Our pleasure!' Rocket, Count, Down and Contact began to bow and smile even more quickly until Fred and Scratch felt quite dizzy.

Fred managed to ask, 'What exactly is Arán's plan?'

'The Creatures from Beyond the Sun will only attack us in the sky. Now, our spaceships are able to cut through very hard things such as the rocks on Glitter... and the

29

earth is very soft compared to those rocks. In fact, my friends have managed to cut a tunnel all the way from the Gaeltacht to here, including going under the great river.'

'Gosh!' thought Scratch. 'A tunnel like that would make a wonderful new highway for wild animals.'

'We are going to continue the tunnel as far as the airport,' said Gladys.

'And what happens then!'

'We attach our spaceships to the wings of a plane. When we are well away from Ireland, we can safely take off for outer space and the planet Mars.'

'That'll never work,' said Fred. 'You'll need to save all your power to take off into space. That means you can't use the invisibility button. The Creatures from Beyond the Sun would see you immediately.'

'Right! And that's where you and Scratch and Arán come into the picture. My spaceship is of little use in space without a radio or properly working controls. And there is no time to fix it so I must leave it here on earth with you.'

'You mean you're giving us the spaceship?' Scratch's eyes widened with delight.

'Yes. There is plenty of power left in it for your needs. You can have the size torch as well. In return, we want you to distract the attention of the Creatures from Beyond the Sun while we make our escape.'

'Do you mean let them chase us while you get away?' Fred felt a sudden return of his nervousness. 'I don't think we can agree to that at all.'

'Oh of course we can agree to it,' said Scratch. 'Don't be such a cowardy custard. Arán and I can fly the spaceship between us. It'll be as easy as falling off an empty match-box.'

5
Escape into Danger

The five spaceships lined up. Engines were switched on. Sharp points, like the tops of pencils, came out of the front of each spaceship. These points began to turn, slowly at first but then more and more quickly, biting into the earth and pushing it firmly to one side so that the tunnel would be safe from collapse.

At first the earth was so soft that no sound at all was heard. Then great heaps of rocks blocked the way and the noise of cutting through them was deafening. But only once did the spaceships slow down. That was when they passed through a huge rabbit-warren, where a carrot-tasting competition was taking place. The judges and the contestants were so amazed at the sight of the spaceships that they forgot to run away.

Scratch opened the window of Gladys's craft. 'Excuse me,' he said politely, 'but are we going in the right direction for the airport?'

'Straight ahead,' a grey-eared *coinín* managed to say.

Very soon the sound of planes was heard but the spaceships continued to dig until they found themselves in a man-made tunnel.

'It's like the one under the road near the supermarket,' said Scratch. 'That means there must be a grating.'

'And there it is,' shouted Fred, pointing to where bright sunlight shone in stripes down into the tunnel. He and Scratch and Arán ran to investigate.

'We'll have to stand on each other's shoulders in order

to see out,' said Scratch. 'Fred, you're the strongest. And Arán is next. I'm the lightest so I'll be top of the pile.'

Fred swayed dangerously as Arán stood on his shoulders and Scratch scrambled up on Arán's shoulders. Scratch was just able to see that they were very close to the edge of the main runway. There was a huge plane waiting to take off.

'We're in luck!' Scratch jumped down and ran back to Gladys. 'There's a jet about to take off, only hurry.'

'The mice of Glitter will never forget what you and Arán and Fred have done for us,' said Gladys.

Scratch suddenly couldn't bear the thought of never seeing her again. 'If you are able to, will you let us know how you get on?'

'I will. That's a promise. Good-bye, good-bye,' and she climbed into Rocket's spaceship.

Scratch sighed deeply. Then Fred caught his arm.

'There's no time for that kind of thing now, Scratch. We have more important things to worry about. I just hope flying a spaceship is as easy as you and Arán imagine.'

'Of course it is!' said Scratch, as he and Arán sat down at the control panel. Fred took his usual seat behind them.

Arán slowly turned the spaceship and headed back down the tunnel to a place well clear of the runway. He tilted the spaceship upwards. The sharp point cut through the ground like a hot knife through butter. Within seconds, they were in the open air.

Scratch scanned the sky. 'There they are,' he yelled, pointing to the dark cloud formed by the Creatures' spaceship. 'And they've seen us too! Okay! Arán, ar agaidh linn!'

Arán pushed the accelerator and the spaceship sped off

at high speed. The dark cloud split into four great spaceships.

Fred looked back at the airport. The jet plane was taking off with a great roar. Four tiny shapes zoomed up out of the grating and under the shelter of the jet's wing,

'The mice from Glitter have made it,' cried Fred.

'Good! Now all we have to do is lose the Creatures, and I think I know who will help us do that.'

The spaceship zoomed back in over the city. The dinged seagull and his friends screamed in rage and rose up in huge flocks to attack it. But when they saw the four larger spacecraft, they turned their attention to them instead.

'This is our sky,' they screamed. 'Where's your permit? Where's your licence? Are you properly insured? Are you properly insured?'

People in the streets heard the noise and stopped to look.

'It's almost as though the seagulls are attacking the clouds,' a young librarian said.

'You read too many books,' her brother said. 'And yet ... and yet ... you just could be right.'

'There's a banana flying around up there as well,' the young librarian said.

'Oh yes,' said her brother, 'along with grapefruit and a slice of melon, I suppose.'

Arán and Scratch roared with laughter. 'We've stopped the Creatures,' shouted Scratch.

'Only for a moment,' Fred warned.

'They won't dare attack us with humans watching us,' said Scratch confidently. 'Gladys was right. We can go back to the Mansion now and let the engines rest after all the power we've used.'

Without having to be told, Arán landed in the shelter of

33

the old oak-tree. He and Fred and Scratch got out and stretched their legs. Arán looked around the ruined house and garden. He said nothing, but Scratch and Fred knew he was as sorry as they were to see it in such a state.

Then a familiar shrill voice made them all jump. 'Back again are we, and with Arán this time?'

'Honestly, you'll be the death of us yet,' grumbled Fred. 'We never know where you'll be next.'

'Now, now,' the magpie reproved, 'don't forget that if it wasn't for me you'd never have got safely to wherever it is you are living now. Where exactly is that anyway? And where are all those shiny little mice from Glitter?'

Between them, Scratch and Fred and Arán told the magpie the whole story and it was so interesting that no one noticed that long afternoon shadows had started to creep across the garden and that hiding among those shadows were Nixer and Jamser, listening to every word that was said.

When the story was finally over, the magpie said, 'And now I suppose you'll be off back to the cottage to explain what delayed you.'

Scratch and Fred looked at each other in horror. 'We never went to see the animals in the farmyard,' moaned Fred.

'What you did was more important,' said the magpie. 'Your grandfather will understand, especially when he sees the spaceship. Do you know, I'd love a spin in a spaceship?'

'You're welcome any time you're passing,' offered Scratch.

'Good!' said the magpie. 'Now where exactly is the cottage?'

'You follow the river out of the city until you reach a

waterfall. The farmhouse is in among a belt of trees. The cottage is a bit further on, two fields away from the river bank,' Fred explained.

'Well, that's easy enough to remember.'

Jamser and Nixer smiled at each other. Indeed it was easy to remember, as easy to remember as the way to the fort where Arán lived. If they didn't catch up with Fred and the Matchless Mice in one place, they could always try the other.

Of course, it would all be made so much more easy if they could get to know the Creatures from Beyond the Sun.

6

The Tough Cats Join In

Arán and Scratch took turns to steer the spaceship through the tunnel.

Fred sat in the back seat, not daring to speak in case he distracted the mice. It seemed like years instead of just a few hours since he and Scratch had set out to talk to the animals in the farmyard. Of course, it was his fault that they had ended up like this. He should have been firmer. After all, he was older than Scratch and bigger, or would be once they were back at the cottage.

The spaceship sped through the great warren. The rabbits heard it coming this time and stood tidily to one side to let it pass. But as soon as it had passed, the grey-eared *coinín* said, 'I'd love to know what's going on. I think I'll go for a bit of a hop.'

Out he went through the most convenient exit and looked around. A very odd-looking cloud was moving quickly across the sky. Then he saw a black cat and a marmalade cat running towards him.

As a rule, the grey-eared rabbit, whose name was Bounce, didn't care much for cats. But there was something about these two cats that made him speak to them.

'Hello there,' he said. 'How's the form? I haven't seen you around here before.'

'Nor will you again,' the black cat said. 'Can you tell us where the river is?'

'Over there.' Bounce pointed. 'What do you want with the river?'

'Friends of ours have gone on a fishing expedition,' the black cat lied. 'Isn't that right, Jamser?'

'It certainly is, Nixer,' the marmalade cat replied.

'Oh, I see. I just wondered if you were after the flying banana,' said Bounce.

Nixer's eyes narrowed to mere slits. 'The flying banana?'

'There was a bunch of them a while back, looking for the airport. Five went out but only one came back. With a cat and two mice in it.'

Nixer and Jamser exchanged looks before Nixer asked in the most innocent voice imaginable. 'Where exactly did you see the flying banana?'

'They dug a tunnel that passed through our burrow.'

'Could we see the tunnel?' asked Jamser.

'I don't think you'd fit down the hole.'

'Oh, cats can fit lots of places you'd never think,' said Nixer. 'Unless of course you're saying that my friend and myself wouldn't be welcome to enter your home?'

'Oh, no, I wasn't getting at that at all.' Bounce knew he was in real trouble now. These cats were tough bullies. 'I just think that I should let the others know you're coming so that they can tidy the place up a bit.'

But when Bounce tried to move, he couldn't.

'What's the matter with you?' growled Nixer.

'I don't seem to be able to move,' whispered Bounce in a terrified voice.

'Can't move?' Nixer tried lifting his own left paw. It remained firmly attached to the ground.

The same thing was true of Jamser. 'It's that Fred and his mice friends. They have some kind of magic.'

'Not magic,' muttered Nixer. 'Mischief.'

'But I've never done anything to them,' wailed Bounce.

At that very moment, a piece of chain bounced off his head.

He and the cats looked up. The thin chain was coming out of the strange cloud. Two more pieces of chain appeared, one above each of the cats. Suddenly the three chains began to go back up into the cloud. Nixer, Jamser and Bounce went up after them, the way a pin might when attracted to a magnet.

'We've been magnetised!' shouted Jamser.

The cloud swirled around them. Figures flickered like shadows on a dark television screen. The three metal chains changed shape. They curved like the earphones on a walkmaster and settled on the ears of the cats and the rabbit.

'Now we're being wired for sound,' screamed Nixer. 'I'm not sure that I wouldn't prefer to deal with a giant-size Fred and Scratch.'

Then they heard The Voice. A very soft voice that in spite of its softness had something very strange about it.

'You must listen carefully to what we have to say,' came through the earphones. 'You are in our power and will stay there unless you help us. Do not remove your earphones. Otherwise you will not be able to understand what we say. Nor will we be able to understand what you say.'

'It must be some kind of speech translator,' Bounce thought.

'That is exactly what it is,' continued The Voice, reading his thoughts. 'It is the latest invention of the new masters of the planet Glitter who have been forced to come to planet Earth to catch their enemies.'

'Do you mean the flying bananas?' asked Bounce.

'We do.'

'You're a bit late. Four of them went to the airport. They must have had a plane to catch. The fifth one is headed west of here.'

'Headed to where?' The Voice demanded.

'To tell you the truth, I'm not sure,' replied Bounce. 'It was travelling so fast I didn't get a chance to ask.'

'We know!' said Nixer, 'or at least we have a pretty good idea of where it is headed. But, first of all, what's going on?'

'You are in no position to ask questions,' The Voice said curtly.

'And neither are you,' said Nixer. 'All we have to do is take off the headphones and you won't be able to speak to us.'

'The headphones not only help us to understand each other,' the voice said. 'They stop you from falling out of the cloud and down on to the earth.'

'This is no time to be argumentative,' snapped Jamser to Nixer. 'Why don't we tell the man what he wants to know?'

'Now you are being sensible, whoever you are,' The Voice purred.

'We're the leaders of the Tough Cat Gang,' said Nixer crossly. 'And we're as anxious to catch up with the flying banana as you are. But we have to get something out of the arrangement as well. We want to take Fred, the cat, prisoner and be able to hunt the Matchless Mice and their friends.'

'That is all right with us,' The Voice said. 'We want only the mouse called Gladys. Once she is in our power, we will have no more problems on the planet Glitter.'

'She must be a very important mouse,' said Bounce.

'She is the only daughter of the leader of the mice on

39

Glitter. That is why she was chosen for this mission to Mars. Her parents felt that as a future leader it was her responsibility.'

'Do you mean she's a mouse princess?' asked Bounce.

'She is certainly the most important mouse on Glitter,' The Voice said. 'But now, rabbit, what do you want from us?'

'I only want to be back down on the ground,' pleaded poor Bounce.

And suddenly he was back on the exact spot where he had first spoken to the cats. His rabbit friends came running out of their burrows.

'What's going on?' they asked. 'Where were you?'

'Up in the clouds,' said Bounce. 'And there is something terrible going on. The leaders of the Tough Cat Gang are planning to destroy Fred and the Matchless Mice. We must find out who Fred and the Matchless Mice are and where they live. It must be somewhere along or near the river. Nixer and Jamser asked me where it was.'

'But in *which* direction along the river?' a serious young rabbit asked.

'Away from the city and airport,' said Bounce. 'That's the direction the flying banana was going. Send out messages while I go and talk to the fish.'

As Bounce hopped off towards the river, the youngest and strongest of the rabbits began to beat their hind legs on the ground. The sound travelled through the maze of rabbit tunnels across the country. It travelled particularly fast along the tunnel made by the spaceships.

Every rabbit who heard it understood what the thumping meant. It was the very special rabbit code.

The message sent by this code was: 'Find Fred and the Matchless Mice. Warn them that the Tough Cat Gang and Invaders from Space are after them. The mice live near the river, near the river, near the river...'

The river? The river! Near the river! Soon the entire countryside seemed to hum with the words. In several places the ground shook slightly.

Grandfather, feeling the ground move beneath his feet, said, 'Hello! What's this then?'

And Flap looked anxiously across the field and said, 'It reminds me of the morning the machines ate the garden around Mangold Mansion.'

'Now, now,' soothed Grandmother. 'There are no machines here.'

'I know but all the same I wish Scratch and Fred were back. They've been gone a long time.'

Grandfather glanced at Grandmother, who glanced at Mrs. Crumbs, who glanced at old Crumbs. None of them spoke but they were all as worried as Flap.

There was another slight tremble under their feet. Alta Attic and several other mice hurried out of the cottage.

'Do they have earthquakes here?' she asked.

'Not that I've ever heard of,' Grandfather said very firmly. 'It's probably just the earth-worms turning the soil over to mark the first day of spring.'

'It's too quiet now for earthquakes,' said Moaner.

And indeed it was suddenly very, very quiet.

On the cloud above the rabbit warren, Nixer and Jamser told The Voice of the Creatures from the Beyond the Sun to follow the river.

'That's where Gladys and the flying banana are headed,' said Jamser.

'We must be careful that they do not see us coming,' The Voice said. 'We shall send you on ahead to spy for us. Hold on to your earphones and away you go.'

The cloud opened. Nixer and Jamser went sliding down a slope of solid bright light into a field not far from the cottage.

'I've never seen a beam of sun as bright as that,' said Grandmother Matchless, pointing to the light coming from the dark cloud.

'Something is going to happen,' Flap declared. 'I can feel it in my bones.'

There was a thunder of hooves from the next field and a sound of barking. Suddenly a dog and a horse stuck their heads over the hedge. 'I'm Shep from the farmyard,' the dog said. 'This is Pull, the horse. Have you any idea where Fred and Scratch are?'

'They left here hours ago to visit you,' said Flap.

Shep looked at Pull. 'Flopsy got it right so.'

'Flopsy?' cried Flap. 'Who is Flopsy and what did she get right?'

'She's the pet rabbit up at the farm. Lives in a hutch by the kitchen door,' said Pull. 'A while ago, a message was sent out by some rabbits near the city about a cat called Fred and a mouse called Scratch and a flying banana.'

'A flying banana.' Flap's voice sounded weak.

'Yes,' said Shep. 'The Tough Cat Gang and some Invaders from Outer Space are after them.'

'Outer Space?' Flap's voice could barely be heard now it was so weak.

'I never heard such nonsense in my life,' said old Crumbs. 'There must be a mistake.'

'Of course,' agreed Grandfather. 'Bananas don't fly.'

'That one does!' Alta pointed dramatically to an object that was at that very moment rising up out of the ditch that surrounded the field in which the cottage stood!

7

The Return to the Cottage

Just when Fred was thinking the tunnel would never end, suddenly they were back to where they had met Arán.

Daylight danced through the overhead branches. After the darkness of the tunnel, the ditch was like a bright valley.

'Almost home now,' said Scratch, as they sped along the ditch. 'Suas linn anois.'

Arán pulled the correct handle. The spaceship rose up out of the ditch.

'Hey, look,' Scratch said. 'It's Shep and the horse talking to Grandfather and the others. I wonder what brought them here.'

'They're all probably been out looking for us,' said Fred.

'Well, when they see the spaceship, they won't be too cross with us,' consoled Scratch.

Fred said, 'We'd better be careful not to frighten them all the same.'

But it was too late to worry about that now, for not only were the mice and animals around the cottage stunned, but all the animals and birds in the hedgerow watched in amazement as the spaceship flew across the field and came to rest outside the cottage.

'I thought it was just a joke until this moment,' said Shep. 'I really did, even though rabbits don't very often make jokes.'

'There is nothing even the tiniest bit funny about this

43

carry-on,' fumed Grandfather. He and Grandmother, with Moaner and Flap close behind, went towards the spaceship, out of which jumped Scratch and Arán and Fred. There was a gasp of horror at how small they were.

Arán tried to put everyone at their ease. 'Conus tá sibh go léir? Nach deas an lá é?'

'Is deas, indeed!' declared Flap. 'Leading Fred and Scratch astray in your spaceship and returning them home only a fraction of their normal size.'

'No, no, you have it all wrong,' cried Scratch. 'It's not Arán's fault.'

'Then whose fault is it?' asked Grandmother.

'We'll tell you the full story in just two seconds, Grandmother,' said Scratch, 'but first we have to use Gladys's torch.'

Scratch pointed the torch at Fred and Arán. There was a flash of blue light and a POP sound. Fred and Arán were back to their usual size!

The gasps of horror turned to gasps of amazement. And the gasps were even louder when Fred pointed the torch at Scratch and Scratch became his usual size as well.

'Now, you've that story to tell us,' ordered Grandfather.

A circle of mice gathered around Scratch and Fred and Arán. Outside the mouse circle, gathered a second circle of wild animals. Birds hovered overhead. Pull leaned as far as he could across the top of the hedge in order to hear. Shep slipped through the hedge and settled down next to a badger. Both of them were so fascinated by the story that they didn't even notice each other.

Neither did they, nor any of the other animals and birds, notice the cold wind that had started to blow or the long dark shadows that had started to creep across the fields.

There was a moment's silence at the end of the story. Then Fred said, 'As you can see, we are safely back home, so all's well that ends well...'

'But it's not ended at all,' Shep cut in. 'The rabbits say the Creatures from Beyond the Sun are still after you.

They think Gladys is still in the spaceship.'

'But they don't know where to find us,' Scratch said.

'Oh, but they do.' Pull sounded gloomy. 'Or did we leave out the bit about Nixer and Jamser?'

'Yes you did,' said Grandfather, 'but put it back in now.'

'Nixer and Jamser are in league with the Creatures from Beyond the Sun. They know you live here.'

There was a stunned silence. Then a shrew muttered, 'I'm off home out of this. It's getting late.'

'And cold,' the badger added. 'Weather can be treacherous this time of the year. I might stay indoors for a few days.'

Within seconds, the birds and the wild animals had all gone.

'Not that I blame them,' said Grandfather. 'Indeed I wouldn't blame Shep and you,' he looked at the old horse, 'if you asked us to move out of here immediately.'

Pull shook his head. 'Better to plan than to panic.' And Shep nodded his head in agreement.

'But we've put you all in danger,' Grandfather pointed out. 'Not that I'm saying that Scratch and Arán and Fred should have done any different under the circumstances.'

There was a long silence. Then Flap suddenly said, 'Sunray!'

Moaner looked at her anxiously. 'Sunray?'

'Yes, Sunray,' repeated Flap in a far-away voice. 'I'm having another feeling in my bones. It's about the bright beam of sun that came through that cloud a while back. Supposing it wasn't a beam. Supposing it wasn't a cloud...'

'Ah now, please, you're frightening the young ones,' reproved Moaner, although it was he himself who was

46

feeling frightened.

'Mother could be right,' said Scratch. 'Pull, you're by far the tallest. What can you see?'

Pull turned his head. He could see across two fields. At first he thought they were empty. Then he saw something move through the shadows.

'There's something moving out there all right,' he reported. 'And I'll bet two buckets of oats it's a couple of cats.'

'Jamser and Nixer!' said Scratch.

'Leave them to me...' growled Shep. 'I'll shift them.'

'It might be better to find out what they are up to,' suggested Fred.

'You're right. I was forgetting that we should plan and not panic. I'd consider it an honour if you'd come with me!'

In spite of the seriousness of the situation, Fred was delighted. 'Just wait till that stuck-up farmhouse cat hears about this,' he thought, as he followed Shep through the hedge.

Scratch started to say, 'Maybe I should go too...' but Flap shook her head. 'Ah, please,' he said.

'The very idea! As though you haven't been through enough adventures to last you for a lifetime... And what about that?' She pointed at the spaceship. 'Is that to be left lying there?'

'Flap is right,' agreed Alta Attic. 'That could be seen from the air.' They all looked fearfully up at the sky. 'It'd be best hidden in the cottage.'

A group of strong, fit mice tested the weight of the spaceship. They had no trouble lifting it. They carried it quickly inside the cottage.

Fred and Shep slipped back in through the hedge. Fred

said, 'It's Jamser and Nixer all right. They have things plugged into their ears and they were giving out directions. Now they've settled down out there to wait.'

'Wait for what?' asked Grandfather

'Well, not wishing to make things seem even worse than they are,' said Shep, 'I'd say they are waiting for the Creatures from Beyond the Sun to arrive.'

'The cloud!' cried Flap. 'Where's that cloud we saw earlier? Is that it over there on top of the hills?'

A thin black cloud lay stretched like narrow black ribbon along the top of the far-away hills. It began to quiver and move. It became bigger and bigger. Then it began to change its shape into that of a huge fist that seemed as though it might touch the moon that could be seen in one half of the sky.

Arán, who had been standing by silently, suddenly commanded, 'Isteach sa teaichín linn go léir! An madra agus an capall chomh maith.'

'Arán wants us all to go into the cottage,' Scratch translated. 'Pull and Shep as well.'

'But surely we're better out in the open than trapped indoors?' argued Shep.

'Arán must have a plan,' replied Scratch.

Pull jumped over the hedge. 'Better plan than panic.'

'And Arán's plans *always* work out,' insisted Scratch, as he and Fred and the remaining mice followed Pull.

Shep hesitated. He didn't care much for being told what to do, except by the farmer. But then neither did he care very much for the idea of being left alone with that great fist looming across the sky. He turned and raced after the others into the cottage, slamming the door behind him. 'Right! Now, what's this plan of Arán's? It had better be good, and quick, for we are in terrible danger.'

48

8
The Creatures Attack

Arán pointed to the spaceship. 'Cuir é sin lasmuigh!'

'But why?' asked Scratch. 'We've only just brought it inside.'

'Deán rud orm, le do thoil. Níl am ar bith le spáráil,' arsa Arán, ag glacadh taobh amháin den spásarthach.

Scratch took the other end, saying to Fred, 'Give us a paw, please. Arán says we are to take the spaceship outside as quickly as possible. We have no time to spare.'

The Always Hungries said, 'We'll help too.'

But Arán, deducing from the way they moved what they wanted to do, shook his head. 'Ní hea, seachas an triúr againne, caithfidh gach éinne fanacht istigh.' Then, with a great heave, he, with Fred and Scratch, carried the spaceship outside.

The fist in the sky was bigger than ever but Arán ignored it. He said to Scratch, 'Measaim gurb é an chaoi a n-oibríonn an tóirse go laghdaíonn gach rud a ndírítear air é chun go mbeidh sé beag go leor le dul sa spásarthach.'

Scratch asked, 'Do you mean the entire cottage?' He swung around to Fred. 'Arán thinks that torch will reduce anything to a size small enough to fit into the spaceship, even the cottage.'

Arán pointed the torch at the cottage. There was a huge flash of white light and a bang rather then the usual popping noise. The cottage, with all those inside it, became as small as the tiniest doll's house.

The fist in the sky began to swoop downwards.

Fred lifted the cottage into the spaceship and put it down carefully on a seat. Arán and Scratch jumped in behind the controls. Within seconds the spaceship was whizzing across the fields to the shelter of the hedge.

Seconds later the fist slammed down on where the cottage had stood. Grass, stones and great sods of earth exploded up into the sky. A great rumble of rage came from the cloud as it swung around in the direction taken by the spaceship.

It stretched out a long finger and pointed it across the fields. A zig-zag of light flashed from the top of the finger and skimmed the top off the hedge as the spaceship dropped down out of sight.

Faint squeaks of terror and alarm came from inside the cottage. Grandfather could be heard calling out, 'What's happening? What's happening?'

Scratch called back, 'We are safely in the ditch now, Grandfather.'

But it seemed that Scratch spoke too soon. Just then another section of hedge was ripped away.

Fred jumped. 'I thought the Creatures from Beyond the Sun didn't want to annoy the humans on earth.'

'Neither do they,' said Scratch. 'But if you didn't know about the Creatures, what would you think was happening right now?'

'A thunderstorm!... I'd think it was a terrible thunderstorm, unlike any ever seen in Ireland before.'

'Exactly. And that's what the Creatures want the humans to think too. But we'll be safe once we get to the tunnel.'

'The tunnel? We're not going to try that trick with the jet plane again, are we?' asked Fred.

'No,' said Scratch. 'We're going to the Gaeltacht with Arán.'

Overhead, the great fist had spread out so that it looked exactly like a huge storm cloud. For miles around, people ran for shelter. Those indoors rang up the radio and television stations and complained bitterly about how wrong the weather forecast had been.

In the farmyard, the animals hoped that Pull and Shep were safe.

In the middle of an empty field, Nixer and Jamser shivered and trembled as the ground beneath their feet shook with the sound of the attack of the Creatures. Branches and rocks fell on top of them. 'We should never have got involved with the Creatures,' groaned Jamser. 'They don't care who they hurt. They might even turn on us next and blame us for the spaceship escaping.'

'And escaping is what we should be doing instead of lying here under this rubble!' Nixer crawled out from under the remains of the hedge. 'Let's see if we can't find that tunnel. I'll bet that's where the spaceship has gone. We'll be safe there.'

'But the Creatures know how to get to the Gaeltacht,' moaned Jamser. 'We told them.'

'Yes, but we can always change sides if the Creatures attack us.'

The cloud was already rising higher and higher up into the sky until it was barely visible.

The two cats ran to what was left of the hedge and followed the ditch until they reached the mouth of the tunnel. It was just wide enough for them to get inside one at a time. They ran and ran and ran. But it seemed to stretch forever.

'It'll take us days to get to the Gaeltacht along this,'

panted Jamser. 'And we have to keep coming up for air.'

'Drainpipes!' shouted Nixer. 'Do you remember Fred and Scratch yelled down the drainpipe at us last Christmas and how loud the noise was? Maybe that'd work in a tunnel as well. Only we'd have to yell something friendly... and yet something that might be a bit of a warning. That way they'll think we're trying to help them!'

'What about the Matchless Mice song?' Jamser hummed a few bars, making sure he had the tune. Then he tried the words. 'We are the Matchless Mice, we are, shining bright, as a shining star.'

'That's it,' remembered Nixer. 'They sang that when they left the Mansion. I remember you and me hearing it and wondering what was going on. If only we'd gone and looked, we'd have been saved all this trouble.'

'Now then, Nixer, no more of that kind of talk. The mice and us are in the same boat now. But what about the warning to go with the song?' Jamser ruffled his fur thoughtfully. 'It'll have to rhyme with "star". In fact, I think I have the answer!'

Jamser carefully stuck his head in the opening of the tunnel and sang as loudly as he possibly could.

> *Matchless Mice is what you are,*
> *Shining bright as a*
> *Shining star.*
> *But the Tough Cats*
> *Know where you are...*
> *AND SO DO THE CREATURES...*

The sound of Jamser's voice went soaring along the tunnel, catching up with and flowing over the spaceship.

'What was that?' asked Fred. 'It sounded important.'

52

Arán and Scratch slowed down and opened one of the windows. Jamser sang the words again.

'That's Jamser!' shouted Fred. 'Do you think it's a trick?'

'No, I don't think it is,' said Scratch, 'But neither do I think we should turn back. If the Creatures know we are headed for the Gaeltacht, we need to get there as quickly as possible and warn everyone.'

The spaceship sped on beneath the countryside and under the great river and past the mountain with the seven bends, until a faint glow of daylight was visible.

Arán, who had been on look-out, suddenly said, 'Táimid ann anois.'

'Prepare for landing,' yelled Scratch to Fred.

Fred held the cottage carefully so that it wouldn't be too shaken when the spaceship landed.

Outside the mouth of the tunnel, the last of the day was fading from the sky. A great carved stone in the shape of an eagle loomed up against the sky. In the shadow of this stone was a fine old castle, out of which a huge crowd of mice ran to watch the spaceship land.

As Arán stepped out of the spaceship, a great cheer went up. The cheer became even louder when Scratch and Fred, carefully carrying the cottage, appeared. Fred put the cottage down in the middle of a large piece of flat ground. Arán pointed the torch at it. The blue flashed and there, back to its full size, was the cottage.

Grandfather and Grandmother Matchless led the others out. 'Where are we at all?' asked Grandfather.

'We are in the fort of the MacLeasa,' said Scratch.

'The fort of the MacLeasa?' Grandfather looked around and saw the fine old castle. 'And do you mean this is our ancestral family home?'

'Yes,' said Scratch, 'I think it must be.'

'Well, well!' Grandfather gave a quick glance at old Crumbs to see how he was taking the news. 'So it seems that we Matchless Mice do indeed come from a very noble background. In fact, I would almost say that compared to this castle, Mangold Mansion was quite a small house.'

'Now, now, Grandfather,' said Scratch. 'We'll have to leave all that until later, for it seems that the Creatures are still after us.'

'You don't mean they will destroy this grand place,' cried Flap. She, like Grandfather, liked the castle very much indeed.

'Ba cheart dúinn dul i gcomhairle le m'athair, Im, an MacLeasa,' a dúirt Arán. 'Is é do sheanuncail é, col ceathrar do sheanathar, uncail le d'athair,'

Scratch hoped he got it right when he explained to the others. 'We are about to meet Arán's father, who is my granduncle, Grandfather's first cousin, and my father's uncle.'

'How confusing!' said Grandmother, as they all tried to work it out.

Then a great silence fell on the crowd as out of the castle there came a fine gray-haired old mouse who had about him a great air of wisdom. It was Im, the MacLeasa.

Arán did the introductions, and Grandfather and the MacLeasa solemnly shook hands.

The MacLeasa said, 'Ócáid mhór í seo gan aon dabht, ag a bhfuil an dá chraobh is gradamúla dár gclanna ag casadh ar a chéile. Tá áthas orm gur thug sibh cuairt orainn ar dheireadh thiar.'

Scratch translated. 'The MacLeasa says it is indeed a great moment when the head of the two most distinguished branches of our family meet. He is delighted that you have at last come to visit.'

Old Crumbs looked as though he was about to say something very rude. Grandmother noticed this and said, 'And of course we mustn't forget the Crumbs Kitchens.'

The MacLeasa had heard all about the Crumbs Kitchens from Arán and said, 'Tá fáilte romhaibhse freisin. Ach creidim go bhfuil rud éigin práinneach le plé.'

'Yes, very urgent,' Scratch lapsed into English in his anxiety. 'There is no time to be wasted.' Then remembering that the MacLeasa spoke no English he used Irish again.

The MacLeasa listened carefully to what had happened. He thought for a moment and said, 'Feictear domsa gurb í an spásarthach atá ag teastáil ó na Créatúir.'

Scratch translated for the others. 'It is the spaceship that the Creatures want.'

'Dá gceapfaidis go mbeadh sí sin scriosta acu, b'fhéidir go ligfidis dúinn, go háirithe dá gceapfaidis go raibh an chuid againn féin a bhfuil eolas againn ina dtaobh curtha ó rath acu,' the MacLeasa continued.

Scratch translated again. 'If they thought they had destroyed that and all who know about them, they might leave us alone.'

'Caithfimid deifir a dhéanamh,' said the MacLeasa.

'An té nach bhfuil láidir ní foláir dó bheith glic.'

'We must work quickly. We must be clever rather than strong.'

'Clever rather than strong!' Grandfather nodded in agreement as Scratch translated.

Scratch listened again carefully to the MacLeasa. Then he turned to the others. 'The mice here make mice dolls for the tourists they've been hoping would come. The cottage will have to be used, I'm afraid, as part of the plan. It will have to be destroyed.'

'And what about the spaceship?' asked Fred. 'Will that not have to be destroyed as well?'

'No: We can use a real banana,' said Scratch with a loud giggle.

'Please be serious,' reproved Flap.

'I was being serious, Mother.'

'And it's a very good idea,' said Pull in his rumbly voice. 'It'll look like a spaceship when seen from the sky.'

'Talking of things from the sky,' added Shep. 'I think a few look-outs would be a very good idea.'

'The eagle rock is the ideal place for look-outs,' said Pull. 'And it had better be mice. Mice will look more normal sitting up there.'

'Let me go,' volunteered Alta Attic, 'I'm used to heights.'

'We'll come as well,' added the Always Hungries. 'Just in case Alta feels lonely. We'll be able to hear what you're saying up there.'

'Well, whatever else has to be said had better be said quickly,' old Crumbs declared. 'For I don't understand the plan at all.'

9

The Plan Works

Grandfather cleared his throat and spoke. 'Once more we find ourselves in great danger.'

Scratch translated for the Irish-speaking mice.

Flap's heart filled with pride at the sight of little Scratch standing between the two senior mice. 'Now aren't you glad he learned Irish,' she murmured to Moaner.

'But we know we can rely on the wisdom of the great MacLeasa, father of Arán, known to some as the cleverest mouse in Ireland,' continued Grandfather.

A great cheer rose as the MacLeasa stepped forward. 'Téimis í mbun oibre láithreach.'

Scratch translated, 'Let us set to work at once.'

'Ní mór na bábóga a shuíomh sa teaichín.'

'The dolls must be placed in the cottage.'

'Ní mór an teaichín a suíomh fad sábháilte ón gcaisleán.'

'The cottage must be placed a safe distance from the castle.'

'Ní mór an bananna a shuíomh lasmuigh den teaichín.'

'The banana must be placed outside the cottage.' Scratch paused for breath.

The mice rushed into the castle and carried out dozens of mice dolls. Grandmother, Mrs. Crumbs and Flap arranged the dolls carefully inside the cottage so that they seemed to be looking out of the windows.

'Save a few for the outside,' said Grandfather.

'What do you mean, "the outside"?' asked old Crumbs.

'You'll see in a few seconds.'

Alta Attic called down urgently from the top of the eagle rock, 'There's a funny cloud moving this way.'

'Quick!' said Grandfather. 'The torch!'

'And we'd all better crowd around the cottage so that the flash of light won't be seen by the Creatures,' said Grandmother.

Once more the mice formed a circle but this time Pull was in the centre of it, standing with his back to the setting sun so that his shadow was absolutely huge. Indeed it covered not only Arán but the front door of the cottage as well. 'You'll not be seen now,' he said

Arán pressed the torch button. The white light flashed, and the cottage full of dolls became small enough for Fred to pick up.

Shep came out of the castle carrying a banana as carefully as if it were the juiciest of bones.

'Tar annseo,' arsa Arán. 'Chuadar taobh thiar den charraig mhór. Bhíodar ansin in aice na farraige agus na trá móire. Seo í an trá ina bhfaca mé na lucha ó Ghlitter an chéad uair. Tóg an teach anseo.'

Fred put the cottage down near the edge of the ocean, and Pull covered it once more with his shadow. Arán pressed the torch. The light flashed and the cottage was back to its normal size.

Grandfather ran forward and placed two dolls outside the cottage. He stuck his pipe in the mouth of one of them. Old Crumbs saw at once what Grandfather was at. He took off his scarf and tied it around the second doll's neck.

'It's you and me,' he said.

'That's right,' said Grandfather. 'And this small one can be Scratch.' He put a third doll in place. Then he looked thoughtfully at Fred. 'Pity we can't fit Fred in.'

'I think you did quite well enough as it is,' said Grandmother. 'And maybe now that you no longer have a pipe, you'll stop smoking.'

Shep dropped the banana in front of the cottage. 'Now let's get out of here.'

'The sea would be quickest and safest,' Pull said. 'Heave hoo and up you all go!'

Shep, Fred and the mice clambered up on Pull's back. Pull went swiftly out into the water until only his head and shoulders were visible above the water. The animals clung to his mane. Cold grey and white waves lapped around them but the waves were the same colour as Pull. With the speed at which they travelled, the Creatures would surely think Pull was a rock.

'After all,' thought Scratch, 'if you can have a rock in the shape of an eagle on land, why can't you have one the shape of a horse in the sea?'

Alta Attic and the Always Hungries had left the eagle rock by now and were running to the old castle.

The four great spaceships of the Creatures came swooping down out of the sky. There was a zip of light from each of them once more, like great flashes of lightning, that joined into one great glow above the cottage and the banana. Then there was a huge bang. The cottage and the banana and half the sand on the strand were blown up into the air.

Some of the sand hit Pull and his passengers as it came back down. Quickly the animals brushed the sand out of their eyes. Where the cottage had been, there was now a great hollow into which the sea water flooded.

The animals looked up at the sky. The spaceships of the Creatures Beyond the Sun were already on their way back to outer space. The final rays of the sun gleamed on them

59

before they vanished from sight.

'Safe!' said Grandfather. 'We are safe!'

'For the moment,' warned Old Crumbs. 'If they ever find out how we tricked them, they'll be back. And where are we going to hide next time? If they can do such damage to a beach, think what they might do to the castle.'

'Do you mean we've brought trouble to the MacLeasas?' asked Grandmother sadly. 'Certainly the beach will never be the same again.'

Scratch turned to Arán. 'We are very sorry for what happened to the beach.'

Arán shook his head and began to talk so quickly that Flap had to help Scratch to translate.

'He's delighted about the beach,' said Flap. 'He says that the Creatures have made a wonderful safe swimming place and marina. Just what tourists want!'

'He's right.' Old Crumbs was staring down at the sea, flowing into the great hollow. 'It's a perfect place!'

'And with the tunnel to get them here, it'll be a knockout,' cried Fred.

'Plus trips around the bay in the spaceship,' added Scratch. Then he paused. 'Oh, but I was forgetting. We won't be here to enjoy all that.'

'Now, now,' said Grandfather, 'I think life in a castle might suit us very well. And I'm sure the MacLeasa would welcome our advice as to how certain things should be organized.'

'Oh, but when will you ask him, Grandfather?' Scratch hardly dared to hope that what he was wishing might come true.

'I'll ask him right now,' Grandfather said. 'Gee-up there, Pull, and don't stop until you get to the castle.'

10
The Future is Decided

The safe return of Pull and the others was an even greater cause for rejoicing than their arrival at the fort had been.

'Beidh féasta mór againn,' said the MacLeasa

'We are going to have a great feast,' Scratch translated.

'While that's being got ready, you and I are going to have a long talk,' Grandfather told the MacLeasa.

The MacLeasa led the visiting mice into the castle, and they all looked around in amazement. They had never seen such splendour. A smiling mouse came forward. 'Más maith libh bhur n-éadaí a altrú don féasta, ta neart cinn le spáráil?'

Scratch said, 'They are offering us fresh clothes for the party. You go and choose. I'll stay here for the conversation between Grandfather and Greatuncle Mac-Leasa.'

The MacLeasa and Grandfather sat facing each other at a great table. At first Grandfather talked and the MacLeasa listened. Then the MacLeasa talked and Grandfather listened.

Then the wise old mice smiled at each other as Flap and Moaner came down the great stone staircase. Flap had on a splendid blue dress. Moaner was wearing a red and gold tunic. Behind them came Grandmother and the Crumbs Kitchens in white and yellow. Then there was Alta Attic in the colours of the sunset. Behind her were the Always Hungries and the rest of the visitors, dressed in as many colours as you will see in the mountains on a fine day.

61

When they were all assembled, Grandfather made a solemn prouncement. 'It is settled. We are to stay here in the castle for as long as we like.'

'Oh, how wonderful!' said Alta. 'But now you and Scratch must get dressed as well.'

Scratch and Grandfather chose tunics of green, white and gold. When they came back to the great hall, they found the MacLeasa and Arán dressed in exactly the same colours.

'What an occasion!' Alta was almost overcome, 'Oh, and look at Shep and Pull!'

The dog and the horse were too big to fit inside the castle but they looked in at the window, delighted with the collars of soft green material that the mice of the fort had placed around their necks.

It was time for the celebration to begin. The MacLeasa nodded at two harpists who began to pluck at their strings for all they were worth. At the same time, they sang a song of such sweetness that everyone felt as though they understood every word of it.

'I never thought I'd enjoy a mouse party so much,' sighed Shep.

'But what about getting back to the farmyard?' asked Pull. 'It must be very late.'

Shep looked up at the sky. It was clear of clouds now and filled with stars that sparkled like diamonds. The moon was full and round and cheese coloured.

'You're right,' said Shep. 'We'd better make tracks.'

'Tracks to where? You forget we came here in a cottage inside a spaceship.'

'Well, we can go back the same way, in the spaceship that is. Let's ask Fred and Scratch.' Shep tapped on the window.

Scratch at once hurried outside. 'There will be food soon... I hope you're not too cold out here.'

'No, we're grand,' said Shep. 'But we just thought maybe we should get back to the farmyard. They'll be out looking for us soon. Could you take us there in the spaceship?'

'Of course I can. Fred'll come too and this might be the ideal time to slip away. Old Crumbs is about to recite *The Mouse Stood on the Burning Cheese* and that takes at least twenty minutes. I'll give Fred the nod to get the torch and the spaceship.'

Within forty-five seconds, Shep, Pull, Scratch and Fred were whizzing along the tunnel.

'I hope you and Shep will come and stay at the new tourist centre,' said Scratch. 'We'd all love that.'

'Well, it could only be for half a day or so. The farmer wouldn't like us to be gone longer than that. He might get nosey and try to find out what was going on, although I must admit he's a nice man.'

'He is indeed,' put in Pull. 'Look at the way he looks after me in my old age. Not many would do that.'

'Oh, I don't know,' said Shep. 'Most humans care about animals. It's those that don't that get the rest a bad name.'

'Do you realize we could have gone back by way of the sky instead of the tunnel now that the Creatures think they've destroyed us?' asked Fred. He suddenly stiffened. 'Or have I spoken too soon?'

Just a few yards ahead a great dark shape completely blocked the tunnel.

'Maybe we weren't as clever as we thought,' murmured Shep. 'Maybe we *didn't* fool the Creatures.'

The shape began to move but not at all in the same way

63

as the Creatures' spaceships. Yet there was something familiar about it.

'It's those two cats with the earphones,' growled Shep.

'You're right! It's Jamser and Nixer. They seem to be stuck in the tunnel.' Scratch slowed down the spaceship and opened a window. 'Hey, you two, have you not caused enough trouble for one day?'

'Oh, please,' Jamser said. 'We're very sorry. We're on our way to apologize for ever getting mixed up with the Creatures from Beyond the Sun. And we did try to warn you that the Creatures were after you!'

Scratch looked at the others. 'What do you think? Should we believe them?'

'Well, there are four of us against two of them,' Shep said. 'And I don't see how we can get past them without

helping them.'

Scratch leaned out of the window. 'Okay,' he said, 'But don't try any of your nasty tricks. Prepare to reduce and enter the spaceship.'

Nixer and Jamser clung anxiously to each other as the white light flashed and the loud POPPING noise was heard.

'Sit between me and Pull... and no funny business,' warned Shep, while Pull added, 'I think we should drop these two rogues off first.'

'Are we not going to the fort of the MacLeasa?' asked Nixer.

'No,' said Fred, 'not until we are absolutely sure that you have changed for the better.'

'Oh, but we have,' whined Jamser. 'We'll even give you a present of the earphones that we got from the Creatures. When you put them on, you can understand any language.'

'Hold on just a second there, Jamser,' objected Nixer. 'If they don't trust us, why should we give them anything?'

'I don't actually see those earphones you're talking about,' said Fred.

Nixer and Jamser put their paws to their necks. The earphones were gone! 'We must have lost them.' Jamser sounded baffled.

'Well,' said Fred, 'it looks as though you'll just have to behave from now on. The magpie will let us know how things go.'

'Prepare for ascent,' cut in Scratch. The spaceship shot up through a hole in the tunnel and out over the ruined garden of Mangold Mansion.

'Leave them at the wrecked car,' ordered Fred.

The spaceship swooped down over the weed-clogged lane. The place was deserted. Fred opened the panel and warned the Tough Cats, 'Walk at least a hundred yards away.'

Jamser and Nixer pushed through the tangle of dead nettles.

'Okay,' Fred said to Scratch. 'Use the torch.'

A flash of blue light restored the cats to their full height. Nixer made at once as if to pounce on the spaceship, but Jamser held him back. 'Remember our promise to be good.'

'We were stuck in the tunnel then,' growled Nixer.

'I know that, but if we don't become friends with the Matchless Mice and Fred we'll never know what's going on.'

'Or get our paws on that spaceship or that wonderful torch,' said Nixer thoughtfully.

'Exactly! Exactly!'

The two cats looked at each other. Slowly two wide cat grins spread across their faces.

'Are you by any chance thinking what I'm thinking?' asked Nixer.

'I have a funny idea that maybe I am, although it was a great pity we lost those earphones.'

For a moment the two cats became very serious again.

'If only we knew where we'd lost them we could go and look for them,' said Jamser.

'Well I have a pretty good idea where that place might be . . . only it might not be too wise to discuss it right now.' Nixer peered meaningfully into the shadows around them. 'You'd never know who might be listening. What with busy-body magpies and rabbits sending messages the length and breadth of the country no secret is safe these days. Best say nothing more for now and just set out in the morning on our search.'

'Do you mean go way back down the country?' asked Jamser.

'I do. After all, we know the way.'

'But it's such a long way and besides . . .' Jamser curled his lips and knitted his eyebrows as though he was afraid he'd said too much.

But Nixer was determined that Jamser should finish what he had been going to say. 'Besides what?' he demanded. 'Come on! Out with it now!'

Jamser still hesitated.

'Don't tell me you've gone soft-hearted?' jeered Nixer. 'Don't tell me you're turning into a goody-goody house-cat? Or worse, a mouse lover?'

'No, no, of course not,' protested Jamser. 'It was just that . . . that I thought maybe we should leave the search for a day or two. I mean it's such a long way . . . Maybe if we had a proper rest.'

'We don't need a rest,' said Nixer. 'Other than our usual night's sleep in the back of the old wrecked car. We are the leaders of the Tough Cat Gang. Or have you forgotten?

'No, of course I haven't forgotten,' muttered Jamser. He climbed into the back of the wrecked car and settled down.

Nixer curled up in the front. 'Right then. So at first light we set off and we don't stop until we get our paws on those earphones again. Agreed?'

'Yes, agreed,' said Jamser, managing to keep a note of sadness out of his voice. And he was feeling sad, not only because of the thought of the long journey back to look for the earphones but also because, even while he and Nixer had been talking about getting hold of the spaceship and the torch, he'd had a sudden wish that everything didn't have to be so tough all the time.

11

A Message from Space

As the spaceship crossed the nightsky, the lights in the city below twinkled like stars. The great motorways thronged with traffic were like golden necklaces stretching across the countryside. Under the light of the full moon, rivers, fields and hills were as bright as day.

'Best put us down in the field next to where the cottage was,' said Shep.

'I've been thinking about that cottage.' Pull spoke very slowly. 'And the hedge and the tunnel. It won't all go unnoticed. I mean it's bound to attract attention... a cottage just vanishing like that.'

'People will think it was destroyed by the storm, just like the Creatures from beyond the Sun want them to think,' argued Shep.

'Yes... but where's the rubble?' asked Pull.

'He's right,' said Fred.' There's always rubble when a house is destroyed like when Mangold Mansion was knocked down.'

'And only one bit of hedge was destroyed,' added Scratch. 'That could look odd as well.'

'And once humans come and start poking around they'll find the tunnel.' Shep's voice was gloomy. 'Especially the children.'

'What children?' asked Scratch.

'The ones who spend their holidays at the cottage.'

'So we were right when we guessed humans sometimes came and stayed there,' said Fred.

'Did we leave that out?' asked Pull.

'Yes, you did.'

'Dear, oh dear. That could have been awkward,'

'It could have been *very* awkward,' Fred sounded cross. 'I'm surprised that Shep here didn't think to mention it. After all, one might say that security is his concern.'

'I would have mentioned it once the fine weather began,' replied Shep, feeling rather embarrassed. 'But you all arrived without any warning. The most important thing was to get you all in safely out of the cold.'

'Of course it was,' said Scratch. 'And Fred didn't mean to sound so ungrateful. And anyway we guessed that humans would come to the cottage sooner or later. We were on our way to ask you about that when we met Gladys.' Just mentioning her name made Scratch look anxiously up to where he hoped Mars was. 'Do you think she's all right?'

'Well, if she isn't there's not much we can do, I'm afraid,' said Shep. 'But we still haven't solved the problem of the cottage and the hedge.'

'The only way we can do that is to replace them.'

'Replace them?' The other stared at Pull. 'How on earth can we do that? They're all in bits, all over the place!'

'Maybe there's a gadget in this thing,' said Pull, looking carefully at the control panel. 'Do we know what all these buttons and handles do?'

'Well that one makes it go up and that one makes it go down. That one opens and closes the door.' Scratch pointed to the different buttons and handles as he spoke.

'What does that one do?' asked Shep.

'Oh, that slows it down, I think,' Scratch pressed the button carefully. The spaceship at once slowed down and seemed to float across the sky.

'Oh, how lovely,' cried Scratch. 'This is what swimming must be like.'

'I hope you aren't going to start that nonsense again,' said Fred.

'I only meant that travelling so slowly is like floating in space. And what's water except heavy wet space?' explained Scratch. He pressed another button that he had never touched before.

The spaceship at once began to turn circles in the sky.

Shep turned green. 'Would you mind putting an end to the circling?' he asked. 'I feel a bit dizzy.'

Scratch levelled out the spaceship.

'That red button up there near the side window.' Pull pointed to it. 'What does that do?'

Scratch pressed the red button and the side window at once became a solid blue colour. Pictures appeared on it.

'It must be what we're flying over.'

'Now why would we need a special window screen to show us that, when we can see just by looking down?' asked Fred. 'Unless, of course, it's for when we are flying above clouds and can't see the ground.'

'Or maybe it's like a video recorder,' said Shep. 'They have one at the farm. They record television programmes on it. Trying turning the button to the left.'

Scratch pressed and turned the button at the same time. Suddenly there was a great rush of pictures, all of them going backwards. They saw the rabbits in the warren, the seagulls in the sky, the cottage being attacked. They even saw Scratch and Fred standing on the river bank pointing at the spaceship.

'It's a recording of all that's happened to us today!' Scratch sounded awed.

'Could be very useful if anyone ever doubts our word,' said Fred, 'but I don't see how it could be useful in any other way.'

'Would you mind turning it back to where it was? Somehow looking at it all going backwards...' Shep's voice trailed away.

'Are you feeling sick?' Fred asked anxiously.

'Maybe just a bit dizzier than a few minutes ago!'

'Oh I'm sorry. I'll set things to right at once.' Scratch pressed the button and turned it to the right. The pictures went forward this time but even faster.

Pull groaned. 'I think I'm feeling a bit woozy now,'

'Just press the button once,' suggested Fred. 'and see if that stops the pictures. Look, like this.'

But as he leaned forward towards the red button he slipped slightly, and in spite of the safety belt banged his head against a panel on the controls. The spacecraft immediately seemed to go out of control. It shot right up into the sky, faster and faster. Shep and Pull closed their eyes and groaned as dark spots and funny lines began to dance before their eyes.

'We're headed for outer space,' yelled Scratch, not sure whether or not he was pleased by the idea.

'But we can't be,' Fred yelled back. 'Gladys said there wasn't enough power.'

'That was before the Creatures from Beyond the Sun went away. They did something to the spaceship, with a laser beam or something, to make it lose power. Maybe now that they're gone the spaceship is working properly.'

'But if we go out into space we'll be at their mercy.' Looking out of the window, Fred could already see half of the world far below. 'And anyway, what would your mother say? Or you father? Or worse, Grandfather?'

'You're right,' sighed Scratch. 'And Arán would never forgive us if we left him behind. And what about Shep and Pull?' He glanced back at the horse and the dog. Their ears were down. Their paws were limp. Their eyes were still closed. 'Even if they didn't have to get back to the farm, somehow I don't think they are ready for space travel.'

'I don't think I'm really ready for it myself,' said Fred. 'Bring us back to earth.'

'I would if I could but I can't. You see I don't know how we started to go out into space in the first place.'

'My head hit that panel. That's what started it. Push it back into place.'

Scratch pushed the panel but it wouldn't move. Clouds of dust and meteorites were zooming past outside now. 'It's stuck!'

'Maybe the radio is working again.'

'The radio? You mean we might be able to talk to Gladys?' Scratch forgot how dangerous things had become and excitedly switched on the radio.

Pull opened his eyes and groaned. 'The Creatures from Beyond the Sun might hear.'

'I don't think they understand without those earphones,' said Fred, 'but just to be on the safe side we'll send out a message in both English and Irish. Gladys understands both.'

Scratch leaned forward and spoke very slowly and clearly into the microphone, 'Spaceship Gladys calling Gladys, Spaceship Gladys calling Gladys.'

Then in Irish he repeated the call, 'Spásarthach Ghladys ag glaoch Ghladys, Spásarthach Ghladys ag glaoch Ghladys.'

There was crackle and a hiss from the radio. Then suddenly they heard, 'Gladys speaking. An tusa 'tá ann a Scratch?'

'Oh yes, Gladys, it is,' cried Scratch. 'An bhfuil tú all right?'

'We are safely on our way to Mars. No sign of the enemy. Níl aon amharc ar ár naimhde. Táimid ar an mbealach slán go Mars. Conas a shocraigh tú an raidió? How did you fix the radio?'

'It fixed itself. It fixed itself.'

'And is the brave and wonderful Fred all right?' asked Gladys.

'Fine... but we're all in a bit of a fix. We seem to be headed for outer space. A panel is stuck.'

'You must press the panel on the opposite side to go back to earth,' advised Gladys.

Scratch tested the panel on the opposite side. It moved slightly. 'Yes, I've found it!'

Fred whispered in his ear. 'Ask her why there's a video recorder on the spacecraft.'

'You ask her. I know she'd love to talk to the brave, wonderful Fred!'

Fred couldn't help feeling pleased as he spoke into the microphone. 'Fred here. Fred here. Over.'

'Oh, you brave and wonderful cat,' said Gladys. 'We will erect a monument to you and Scratch.'

'Oh, that's very good of you, but the thing I'm asking about now is why is there a video recorder on the spacecraft?'

'Oh, so that we will have a record of our journeys, and also in case there is anything that needs to be corrected,' Gladys said.

Shep opened his eyes. 'Corrected? Fred, I think you're on the right track.'

Fred felt even more proud now. 'Does that mean you can put things right, Gladys?'

'Yes ... if it's the right thing to do.'

'Could we put the cottage and the hedge back?' asked Fred. 'They both were destroyed by the Creatures.'

'Just find the place on the videotape where that happened,' commanded Gladys.

Shep closed his eyes again while the tape was wound backwards.

'We have the place. We have the place,' shouted Scratch.

'Directly in front of you, under the pilot's seat, is a handle.'

'I have it! I have it!'

'Then press it down ... press it down.'

As Scratch pressed, Fred looked on intently. Shep and Pull opened their eyes. The pictures on the screen began to go backwards by themselves. The pieces of the hedge fell back into place. Then the pieces of the cottage fell back

74

into place. They both looked as they had looked before the day's adventures began.

'That's truly remarkable!' murmured Shep. 'I don't think I've ever seen the equal of that anywhere.'

'No more than I have,' added Pull. 'But should we not be getting back to the farmyard?'

'Oh, yes, of course we should. I almost forgot... Scratch here... 'a Ghladys, caithfimid imeacht anois. Caithfimid imeacht!'

'I will be in touch soon,' said Gladys. 'Good-bye, Scratch. Slán, oh wonderful Fred. Here is music to guide you on your way.'

As Scratch pressed the other panel and turned the spaceship back towards the earth, music came through the radio and filled the cabin. A voice that sounded like that of Gladys began to sing.

> *Here's to our friends on earth:*
> *To Fred and Scratch*
> *And Pull.*
> *To Shep and all*
> *Those mice who only*
> *Do us good.*
> *Their names will never die in space.*
> *And in the heavens above*
> *We'll write their names in shining*
> *Stars for all to read and love*

Words began to appear right across space... SCRATCH, FRED, PULL, SHEP, ARÁN, GRANDFATHER, GRANDMOTHER, FLAP, MOANER, AND ALL THE OTHER MICE INCLUDING THE GREAT MACLEASAS.

Under the names appeared the words. 'Go n-éirí an bóthar libh go léir.'

12
Down to Earth

The spaceship cruised gently across the countryside. It passed over the cottage and the hedge, both looking as though nothing had ever happened to them.

'Best let us out in the field by the river,' advised Shep. 'We can get back to the farmyard easily from there.'

The spaceship glided to a halt in the middle of the field. Scratch and Fred jumped out first, then Pull and Shep.

'Well, it's time for us to be restored to our normal size,' said Shep, 'and there's no need to worry about the Creatures seeing the torch this time!' Then he went on point. 'Hey, now! What's that over there?'

He went jumping through the grass until he reached an object on the ground. 'It's the earphones those cats had. They must have dropped them when the hedge was blown up.'

'That means we can listen in to what the Creatures are doing,' cried Scratch.

'We might even be able to talk to each other if we can learn how they work.'

'Ask Gladys next time you speak to her,' said Pull.

'We will,' promised Fred. 'In the meantime, you take one set and we'll keep the other. Pity we don't have two torches. That would make everything perfect.'

'Two spaceships might be even more perfect,' neighed Pull.

'Now, now,' reproved Shep. 'Let's not get greedy. We've done very well. There's just one thing I'd like to do sometime, and that's borrow the video.'

'I suppose that's to prove to that farmhouse cat that it all really happened,' Fred said. 'You can have the video now if you like.'

'Safer to take it later in case the farmer hears us coming back so late,' said Shep. 'It might be safer too to hide our set of earphones over here in the ditch and collect them in a few days time!'

Scratch pressed the torch button. The blue light flashed, and Pull and Shep were back to their proper size.

'Good-bye,' shouted Fred and Scratch. 'See you soon.'

'Good-bye, good-bye. Safe journey,' Shep and Pull replied, watching as the cat and the mouse ran back to the spaceship. They waved as the spaceship took off and sped away into the night.

'Do you know,' said Pull. 'I think we're in for a right bout of adventures and travels, what with spaceships and earphones.'

'And do you know,' said Shep. 'I think you might be right there.' He picked up the set of earphones and dropped them into the ditch. 'They'll be safe there.'

The bright moonlight turned the river the colour of silver. Far down below Fred and Scratch could see Shep and Pull hurrying back to the farmhouse.

'Our names in the stars,' said Fred. 'Will everyone be able to see them, do you think?'

'I don't think so somehow,' said Scratch. 'Only those who want to.'

Back in the city, Jamser stirred in his sleep. Then suddenly he was wide-awake, staring at the sky through a hole in the roof of the wrecked car. For a second he thought he was imagining things. But no, there were definitely names twinkling away up there! He was about to waken Nixer but he knew Nixer would be too cross to look. He settled back down and tried to go to sleep again but couldn't.

At last the new day began.

Nixer jumped out of the wrecked car. 'Right!' he said. 'Off we go!'

Jamser trailed after him as best he could. By the time they reached the river he was exhausted.

'Come on,' said Nixer. 'There's a road running alongside the river. All we have to do is take a lift.'

A lorry slowed down at traffic lights. Nixer and Jamser jumped into the back of it and were bounced around like a couple of footballs until suddenly Nixer said, 'Out, out! There's the field.'

They landed in a pile of thorny bushes.

Jamser looked through the hedge. 'This can't be the field,' he said. 'There's no damaged hedge.'

'Then it's the next field,' said Nixer crossly, picking a thorn out of the tip of his tail.

But there was no damaged hedge in the next field either. Or the next. Or the next.

'All the fields look the same,' said Jamser. 'And the river looks the same too.'

'All we have to find is the damaged hedge and the blown-up cottage. There can't be many of them around.'

'What about that cottage there?' Jamser pointed to a cottage in the middle of the field they had just climbed into.

'That's an UNEXPLODED cottage,' said Nixer. 'And the hedge we've just come over is an UNEXPLODED hedge.'

'I'm not so sure... I think it's the cottage where the mice and Fred lived.'

'Now how can it be the same cottage?' asked Nixer.

'Well, I'm staying there,' said Jamser.' I've had enough of rushing around and causing trouble and sleeping in old cars. I want my name in the stars too.'

Nixer looked very anxiously at Jamser. 'What are you saying?'

'You heard what I said,' declared Jamser. 'Now you can go or stay, please yourself.'

With that Jamser ran towards the cottage. The door was open and the inside was full of warm sunshine. He curled up in a corner and went fast asleep.

Nixer looked around. Suddenly he was all alone and forced to admit that he had no idea where he was. He suddenly felt very lonely. But he hated to admit he was wrong or that Jamser had meant what he had said.

'Maybe when he's had a bit of a rest he'll feel better,' he thought. 'Maybe I'll just wait outside the cottage until he wakes up.'

Nixer stretched out in the warm sunshine. He could hear a bee buzzing somewhere. It was a very nice sound. In fact the fresh air was very nice too. His eyes closed. His head touched his front paws. He began to dream the happiest dream he had ever known.

Tony Hickey

Tony Hickey was born in Newbridge, County Kildare, where he grew up.

After a time spent in educational film-making and radio and TV drama, he first began writing for children in the BBC's *Jackanory* programme and RTE's *Storyroom*. He also worked on *An Baile Beag* and *Wanderly Wagon,* and has dramatized several children's classics for radio including *The Wizard of Oz, The Lost Prince,* and Patricia Lynch's autobiography, *A Storyteller's Childhood.* He is at present working on a pilot for a new TV series and on a radio play for Radio Éireann.

This is the third of the Matchless Mice stories. The others were *The Matchless Mice,* and *The Matchless Mice's Adventure,* both with illustrations by Pauline Bewick. Also for The Children's Press, he has written *The Black Dog,* an adventure story set in the countryside of his boyhood.